SPECIAL EDITION

CHEWY
AND CHICA

THE PUPPY PLACE

**Don't miss any of these
other stories by Ellen Miles!**

THE PUPPY PLACE

SPECIAL EDITION

CHEWY AND CHICA

ELLEN MILES

SCHOLASTIC INC.

New York   Toronto   London   Auckland
Sydney   Mexico City   New Delhi   Hong Kong

For my writing buddies

Norma, Leda, and Linda,

with love and thanks.

ISBN: 978-0-545-20024-0

Cover art by Tim O'Brien
Original cover design by Steve Scott

12 11 10 9 8 7 6 5 4 3 2 1   10 11 12 13 14 15/0

Printed in the U.S.A.   40

First printing, May 2010

CHAPTER ONE

Date: April 22

Time: 4 P.M.

Event: Caring Club, first meeting

President: Lizzie Peterson

Notes by: Lizzie Peterson

Others in attendance: Charles and Betsy Peterson, Maria, Ms. Dobbins, Julie (shelter employee), Sammy.

Ms. Dobbins and Lizzie opened the meeting with an explanation of what the Caring Club is all about. Our mission is to learn about the best ways to care for and help our animal friends, to educate the public about animals and pets, and to do good deeds for our community. History of the club: Lizzie read about another Caring Club in some other town and asked Ms. Dobbins if they could start one at Caring Paws Animal

Shelter, where Lizzie volunteers. (Lizzie is president because the whole thing was her idea.)

Lizzie's younger brother Charles has joined, and their mother, Betsy, will also attend meetings as often as possible, as long as she doesn't have to watch their younger brother, Adam, also known as the Bean, who might be too squirmy to sit still through a whole Caring Club meeting. The Petersons are all very familiar with the problems pets face, since they are a foster* family for puppies.

Maria is Lizzie's best friend and also an animal lover, although she loves horses best of all. Sammy is Charles's best friend, who lives next door.

Meeting continued with a brainstorming session about things the Caring Club could do. For example:

— Write informative letters to the editor of the newspaper about pets and how to care for them properly. (Like not leaving them in your car when it's warm out.)

— Be kind to every dog and cat (and horse) we meet.

*Definition of fostering: taking care of puppies who need homes, just until the perfect forever family is found for each one.

— Teach our own pets (for example, the Petersons' puppy, Buddy, the cutest, sweetest dog ever) how to be good canine citizens with nice manners.

— Have a bake sale or a dog wash (like a car wash, only with dogs) or something else to raise funds for Caring Paws.

— Take our well-behaved dogs to schools and workplaces to show off their manners and maybe also some tricks they can do, like —

4:30 P.M.: Meeting suddenly adjourned. Explanation later.

It was just as well that Lizzie decided to give up on taking notes, since no matter how fast she scribbled, it would have taken her way too long to write down everything that happened that spring afternoon in the middle of the first Caring Club meeting.

What happened was this. First there was a knock on the door. "Ms. Dobbins?" Andrew, the boy who worked at the front desk of the animal shelter, poked his head in. His cheeks were flushed pink and he stumbled over his words.

"I — I think you might want to come see what just arrived."

Ms. Dobbins stood up. "Thank you, Andrew," she said.

There was something in Andrew's face that made everybody else stand up, too, and follow Ms. Dobbins out to the parking lot in front of the shelter. There Lizzie saw a big shiny black car, pulled up at an angle to the front door. The car's windows were rolled down just a bit. Lizzie couldn't believe what she was seeing, so she stepped forward to take a closer look. That car was full of puppies! Puppy noses stuck out of every window, sniffing and snuffling and snorting. Puppy paws pressed against the glass. Lizzie saw brown puppies, white puppies, and black puppies; fluffy puppies and sleek puppies; big puppies and tiny puppies. Lizzie had never seen so many puppies in one place!

The car door opened, and a tall, gangly man unfolded himself from the front seat, holding back three puppies that tried to climb out after him. He wore worn, faded overalls, with a clean white shirt underneath. He wasn't handsome — in fact, he was kind of funny-looking — but there was something about him that Lizzie liked right away.

He tipped his red baseball cap and smiled at Ms. Dobbins. "Hello, ma'am," he said.

"Mr. Beauregard?" Ms. Dobbins stared at the car, and at the man, and at the puppies. "What is this?"

The man pushed back his cap, scratched his head, and smiled shyly, and Lizzie found herself smiling back at him. "Puppies," he drawled in a Southern accent. "A whole passel of puppies."

"I can see that." Ms. Dobbins turned to the others. "Mr. Beauregard is new to town but he has already become a very generous supporter of Caring Paws."

Lizzie knew what that meant. He might not look it, but this man was R-I-C-H. And he loved animals. That was good! Caring Paws always needed money for dog food and cat litter and flea shampoo and veterinarians' bills.

"These are some other friends of the shelter." Ms. Dobbins swept a hand toward the members of the Caring Club. "And I think we *all* want to know what you're doing with a carload of puppies."

"I bought 'em! I bought the whole lot from a man selling puppies out of a big white truck with red stripes on it, down on Route Nine. I couldn't stand to see the little critters being sold like they were apples or corn at a farm stand. So I gave the man every cent in my pockets and I told him I never wanted to see him around these parts again."

Ms. Dobbins frowned. "I've seen that truck. It makes me so mad that someone would sell puppies that way. I've called the authorities but they say there's no law against it."

"Why is it so terrible?" asked Sammy. "If I was driving past that truck with my mom or dad, I'd want to stop and get a puppy."

"That's exactly it," said Ms. Dobbins. She began a lecture that Lizzie had heard many times before. "If you want to add a pet to your family, there's lots to think about. You need to be sure you're ready for the responsibility. Once you've talked it over, you can adopt a pet from a shelter or buy one from a responsible breeder. But buying a puppy from a truck, just on the spur of the moment — that's not a good idea."

Mr. Beauregard let out a big booming laugh. "That's for sure," he said. "As soon as I did it, I thought, 'Now what, Daniel?' I'd love to keep every one of these rascals myself, but I'm always travelin' for business. Then I figgered out that you'd know what to do, so I drove the whole bunch of 'em over here." He ducked his head and smiled guiltily at Ms. Dobbins. "Course I'll cover any extra costs you rack up taking care of the little peanuts."

"Well," said Ms. Dobbins, "I guess we'd better start sorting them out."

While Lizzie and the others watched, Ms. Dobbins, Mr. Beauregard, Andrew, and Julie began to unload the puppies. First Ms. Dobbins pulled a chunky black Lab pup out of the back-seat. She handed the pup to Andrew, who headed into the shelter to find an empty kennel. Mr. Beauregard got into the car and passed along a shaggy white pup that looked a lot like Snowball, a feisty West Highland white terrier Lizzie's family had once fostered. Then came three puppies in a row: another Lab, a squirmy dachshund, and a sort of beagley looking brown-and-white dog whose long, droopy ears reminded Lizzie of Patches, another foster puppy. "Oh, he's cute!" said Lizzie.

The puppy sneezed. "Cute, yes," said Ms. Dobbins. "But there's a good chance this puppy might be sick, too. I think these puppies came from a puppy mill."

Mr. Beauregard nodded. "A few of these pups are in need of some TLC."

Lizzie knew what TLC meant: tender loving care. But even though she had heard of a puppy mill before, she wasn't exactly sure what it was. She knew that paper was made at a paper mill, and steel was made at a steel mill. So . . . "A puppy mill?" she asked. "What's that? Like a factory for puppies?"

Ms. Dobbins sighed. "Exactly. People who run puppy mills keep mother dogs in cages and make them have litter after litter of puppies, just so they can sell them." She started to talk faster and more loudly, the way she always did when she was upset about something having to do with animals. "The puppies grow up with very little exposure to people, in overcrowded conditions, where diseases can spread easily. The puppies are sold at pet stores, or through classified ads, to owners who don't know that they may be buying a sick dog, or a mixed-up puppy with behavior problems that can't be solved." Now Ms. Dobbins looked really sad. "There are already plenty of unwanted puppies in the world, and we don't need more. Puppy mills are a terrible, terrible thing."

"But . . . aren't they illegal?" Mom asked. She held the dachshund and rocked it like a baby. "They must be. How could anyone treat dogs that way?"

"They're banned in some places, but not in this state. Our legislature hasn't passed a law against puppy mills yet," Ms. Dobbins said. She sighed and went back to unloading the car.

The puppies just kept coming. Andrew and Julie took the dogs into the shelter and settled them into kennels. Lizzie saw a tiny long-haired shih tzu, a German shepherd with huge ears and a pointy nose ("That looks just like Scout when she was a puppy," Charles said when he saw it), and another Lab puppy, a yellow one this time. Lizzie wished she could hug and kiss and hold every single one of them, but Ms. Dobbins wanted to get them settled as quickly as possible.

"We're out of kennels," reported Andrew after he'd taken the yellow Lab puppy inside.

"I was afraid of that," said Ms. Dobbins. "And there are still two puppies left. Brother and sister, by the looks of them."

She reached into the car one more time and Mr. Beauregard handed over two teeny, tiny puppies. Their heads were shaped just like apples, and both had short fur, perky ears, and big, bulgy shiny brown eyes. "This one is the boy" — Ms. Dobbins held up a brown-and-white one — "and this one is the girl." She showed off a black-and-white one.

Lizzie could hardly believe how small they were. They snuggled together, fitting perfectly into Ms. Dobbins's cupped hands. Lizzie couldn't help herself. She walked right over to Ms. Dobbins and put out one finger to gently pet the black-and-white puppy's tiny head.

"Chihuahuas!" said Lizzie.

"You're absolutely right," said Ms. Dobbins.

CHAPTER TWO

Lizzie was *always* right about dog breeds. Charles knew that it was because of the "Dog Breeds of the World" poster in her room. She had practically memorized it, so even if she had never seen a briard in real life, she could tell you exactly what it looked like (huge, shaggy), where it came from (France), and what it was used for (guarding sheep). Charles had to admit that Lizzie knew a lot about dogs.

"Chihuahuas who are going to need a foster home," Ms. Dobbins went on. She looked right at Mom when she said that.

Mom gulped. "Two puppies?" she asked. "You want us to foster two puppies at once?"

Ms. Dobbins nodded. "These two will probably do best if they are together for now," she said. "They may have to be separated eventually, but I hate to do it on their first night in a new place. If you could just take them for a few days, until I find homes for some of the other puppies . . ."

Sammy nudged Charles. "C'mon, you have to take them," he whispered.

"We'll do it!" said Charles.

Mom turned to him. "But what about our trip?"

"Never mind the trip," Lizzie burst out. "This is way more important."

Charles bit his lip. He had almost forgotten about the vacation his family had been planning for the last few weeks.

The Petersons planned to leave Buddy with Charles and Lizzie's aunt Amanda, who ran a doggy day-care center, then drive up to AdventureLand, the coolest amusement park ever. Charles had looked forward to it all spring. He'd even saved up his allowance for extra ride tickets. He planned to try to set a world record for riding the roller coaster.

Charles looked at the puppies. The brown-and-white one trembled and shivered. Was he cold? He cocked his head and blinked up at Charles.

What's going on? Who's going to take care of me? I'm so scared!

"Why is he shaking like that?" Sammy asked.

"Chihuahuas are known for shivering and trembling," Lizzie said right away. But Charles could tell she didn't know why.

"They shiver for all sorts of reasons," explained Ms. Dobbins. She tucked the puppy in closer to her chest. "Sometimes they tremble because they're excited, and sometimes because they're scared. They also get cold very, very easily, because their coats are so short. It's up to the owner to figure out why they're shivering and help make them feel better."

"Kind of like when the Bean was a baby and he'd cry and cry and we had to figure out if it was because he was hungry or had a wet diaper or if maybe something was hurting him?" Charles asked.

"Exactly," said Ms. Dobbins. "In this case, I think maybe our little boy here was feeling insecure. See how he stopped shaking when I held him closer?"

Sure enough, the puppy's body was still now. He gazed up at Charles with his big, bulgy brown eyes.

Ms. Dobbins raised her eyebrows. "Well, now that you've had your first lesson in Chihuahuas, what do you think?" she asked. "If you can't take them, I'll have to start making some calls. But it won't be easy to find someone who can foster both puppies."

Charles took a deep breath. He would hate to see those two puppies go to two different homes. He could tell by the way they snuggled up together that they loved each other. "Lizzie is right. Forget about our trip. These puppies need us. We'll take them."

Mom gave him a look — the kind of look that meant, "Hold on there, buddy! You're not the family decider."

Oops. "I mean . . . can we please, please, please foster these puppies?" asked Charles.

"I should at least call your dad. . . ." Mom began.

"He'll say yes; you know he will." Charles knew that his dad would agree. For one thing, Dad loved puppies. For another, he didn't even like amusement parks. He always said roller coasters made him feel "oogy." He would probably be happy if he didn't have to drive all the way up to AdventureLand.

Mom took another look at the puppies in Ms.

Dobbins's arms. She sighed. "Ordinarily, I would say no. Two puppies — when we already have Buddy at home — it just seems like too much. But now that I know about puppy mills, I know these puppies have had such a hard beginning. They really need our help, don't they?"

Ms. Dobbins nodded. "They really do." The two puppies in her hands squirmed until they were all smushed up together. The brown-and-white puppy gnawed on his sister's tiny ear while the black-and-white one put a miniature paw on her brother's teensy nose. Charles wondered how anything could be so *small*.

"Awww," said Mom. "How can I resist? We'll take them."

"All right!" Charles reached out for the pups.

"Wow! They're so light!" he said when Ms. Dobbins handed them over. The puppies hardly weighed a thing. It was like holding two butterflies. He looked down at them. Two sets of huge brown eyes blinked back up at him. He leaned over to kiss the puppies. The brown-and-white one chewed on his chin while the black-and-white one licked him gently. Both of them scrabbled at his face with their tiny paws.

Hello! Hello! Hello!

Want to be my friend? Please?

"These puppies might be a real handful," Ms. Dobbins warned. "Chihuahuas are not the easiest dogs to train."

Charles hardly listened. He stared down at the adorable puppies in his arms.

"Also, Chihuahuas are very delicate, because they are so small. They can get hurt easily. You have to really keep an eye on them so they don't get stepped on, or fall and hurt their heads." Ms. Dobbins paused. "And you might want to keep them separate from Buddy, and from the Bean, at least in the beginning. Chihuahuas don't always get along so well with other dogs or small children."

"We're always careful about that with our new foster puppies," said Mom.

"I know," said Ms. Dobbins. "Why am I fussing? You Petersons are the best foster family I've ever had. Have a great time, and call me if you have any problems." She waved as she headed back into the shelter to look after the other puppies.

A moment later, Andrew popped back out. "Ms. Dobbins thought you might need extra stuff, with two puppies to care for," he said. He gave Mom two tiny collars and two leashes.

Lizzie came over to Charles. "Don't I get to hold one of the puppies?"

"That's a good idea," said Mom. "Each of you should take one and hold it very carefully as we drive home, since we don't have our puppy crate in the back of the van today."

Charles looked down again at the puppies in

his arms. He hated to let one of them go, even for a minute. The brown-and-white one chewed on the black-and-white one's tiny tail, which made the black-and-white one squeak. They were so cute he could hardly stand it. Should he give Lizzie the brown-and-white boy or the black-and-white girl? While he thought about it, the brown-and-white puppy reached up its paw and touched him gently on the chin. Charles felt his heart melt. He handed the black-and-white puppy to Lizzie.

Immediately, both puppies started to yip and whine.

Wait! Where are you taking my brother?

Come back! Come back! What are you doing with my sister?

The brown-and-white puppy squirmed and struggled, trying to get out of Charles's grasp. He nipped at Charles's fingers — *hard*. His teeth might be tiny, but they were as sharp as needles. It really hurt, but Charles did not want to yell at the poor puppy. "Hold on there, cutie," he said. "Your sister's not going anywhere. Don't worry."

He and Lizzie got into the van, still holding the squirmy puppies, and Mom helped them buckle in next to each other in the backseat. The puppies calmed down as soon as they could see each other. Charles and Lizzie put on their collars and snapped on their leashes. "I guess Ms. Dobbins was right," said Mom. "These two really do like to be together."

By the time Mom got into the driver's seat and started the van, Charles's puppy had begun to gnaw on his own leash. "You're a little chewer, aren't you?" Charles asked as he carefully untangled the leash from the puppy's sharp teeth. Charles could not believe how big and shiny the puppy's eyes were. He looked so innocent as he blinked up at Charles.

Did I do something wrong?

"Wait!" Charles sat up straight in his seat as Mom drove down the road. "We forgot to ask what their names are."

Lizzie looked down at the puppy in her own arms. "I'm sure they don't have any names, since they came from a puppy mill. But Ms. Dobbins always says we can give our foster puppies temporary names."

Charles thought for a second. He loved to name puppies. Maybe since there were two of them, they should have matching names. "How about Ping and Pong?"

Lizzie raised an eyebrow. "I don't think so. They're dogs, not white plastic balls."

Charles thought some more. "Pip and Squeak? 'Cause they're so little?"

"That's cute," Mom said from the front seat.

But Lizzie shook her head. "We can think of something better," she said. "Anyway, let's get to

23

know them first. Then we can find names that fit their personalities."

Charles stroked his puppy's tiny ears. "These puppies are so cute. I bet we'll find them forever homes really soon."

"I hope you're right, Charles," said Mom as she pulled into the driveway at home. "We really have our work cut out for us. These two plus Buddy equals a whole lot of puppies."

CHAPTER THREE

As Mom parked the van, Lizzie looked down at the tiny black-and-white puppy in her lap and shook her head. She still couldn't believe what had just happened back there at the shelter. For years and years and *years* she had begged her parents to let her have a puppy. It had taken her forever to convince them to be a foster family for puppies, and *twice* forever before the Petersons got a dog of their very own. Now pretty much all Charles had had to do was say, "Please?" and Mom had agreed to take two at once. At first, Lizzie was steamed. It wasn't fair. It wasn't right. It wasn't — wait! Lizzie stopped herself before she said a single word out loud. Was she crazy?

No matter how it had happened, the fact was that her family was going to be fostering these two tiny puppies. That was *good* news. Even though Lizzie was usually more of a big-dog person, the truth was that she loved all puppies. And she could already tell that these two mini-pups were going to be maxi-fun.

The puppies started to yip and yelp as soon as the van door opened. "They know they're home," said Lizzie. As soon as they got out of the van, Lizzie's puppy pulled her right over to the bushes by the side of the driveway. "Look, she even knows where to pee." Lizzie bent down to pet her puppy. "What a good puppy. Who's a good, good girl?"

Charles's puppy peed, too.

Then they led the dogs up the walk. When Mom opened the front door, there was the Bean to welcome them home. "Uppy!" the Bean yelled. Next to him, Buddy jumped up and down, barking at the puppies.

"Oh, no." Lizzie tried to hold her puppy back, but the tiny black-and-white girl ran straight at Buddy. So did her brown-and-white brother. Their leashes tangled around Buddy's legs as they dashed back and forth beneath him. Buddy looked enormous next to the tiny puppies. The black-and-white puppy yipped and yapped while the brown-and-white boy chomped at Buddy's ankles. Buddy had stopped barking. Now he looked up at Lizzie with a pleading expression.

Help! Who are these ridiculous little insects, and why did you bring them here?

Mom had scooped up the Bean right away. "No uppies for the Bean," she told him. "These uppies need to be left alone. Charles and Lizzie will take care of them, okay?"

"Uppy!" the Bean wailed and reached out both arms.

"What is going *on* here?" Dad came into the hallway, drying his hands on a dish towel. "What's all that yapping?"

Lizzie grinned. "We have two new puppies to foster!"

"I can see that." Dad smiled down at the wild puppy pile at his feet. "And hear it." The black-and-white puppy was still yipping and yapping her head off. "Quiet down, you! What breed are they?" he asked.

"They're Chihuahuas," Lizzie told him. She kissed her puppy. "Did you know that the Chihuahua breed originally comes from the state of Chihuahua, in Mexico?" She had just remembered that fact from her poster. "Aren't they cute?"

"They're adorable." Dad stepped back. "Except for the barking. But what about our trip?"

"We decided we'd rather foster these puppies. Charles didn't think you'd mind," Lizzie said.

Dad scratched his head. "Well, I guess that's true. I've got plenty to do around here. But . . . *two* puppies? Plus Buddy? How will we manage?"

"I've been thinking about that," said Mom. "We'll all help, but I think the best way is for Charles and Lizzie to each be in charge of one puppy. They'll have to be sure that their puppy gets fed, and trained, and taken outside to do its business."

"I want uppy, too." The Bean pouted and stuck his thumb into his mouth.

"How about if we put you in charge of Buddy?" Mom asked. She winked at Lizzie and Charles. They all knew Buddy was so well behaved that he didn't really need anyone in charge, but it would make the Bean happy to think he had a job. Sure enough, the Bean loved the idea. He laughed and waved at Buddy from Mom's arms.

"I in charge of you, Buddy. Sit!"

Obligingly, Buddy sat. The Bean laughed again. Mom put him down, and he and Buddy raced off toward the kitchen. Buddy's tail wagged madly as he ran. He loved the Bean, and he was obviously happy to get away from the puppies.

Lizzie had been thinking. She liked the idea of being in charge of one of the puppies, and she was already in love with the black-and-white puppy in her arms. "I want this one," she said. "And I'm going to call her Chica. That's Spanish for 'girl.'"

Charles hugged the brown-and-white puppy. "This one's mine, then. And I already thought of a name for him, too. Chewy. Because he's always biting and chewing."

"And can we each also be in charge of finding our puppy its forever home?" Lizzie asked. "Because I'll bet it'll be easy to find a home for Chica." She kissed the black-and-white puppy's head again. The puppy was still yipping, but she stopped for a moment and kissed Lizzie back. "As

30

soon as I teach her not to bark so much, that is."
She set the puppy down on the floor.

"I bet I can find Chewy a home first," said
Charles.

"Oh, you do, do you?" Lizzie asked.

"Yeah!" Charles nodded. "I do."

"Fine," said Lizzie. "Then let's make it a real
bet. First one to find their puppy a home doesn't
have to —" She stopped to think for a second.
What chore did she dislike most? "Set the table
for a whole month," she finished.

"Or clear it, either!" said Charles. "You're on."
He stuck out a hand and they shook on it, with
Mom and Dad for witnesses.

Ha! Lizzie knew she'd win this bet, no problem. She could already tell that Chewy had a
real biting problem. That had to be fixed before
anyone would adopt him, and Charles wouldn't
have a clue how to do it. Meanwhile, so what if
Chica was kind of yappy? Lizzie had trained
other dogs not to bark, like Cody, the wild

Dalmatian puppy the Petersons had fostered. And as soon as Chica quieted down, she'd be very, very adoptable. Who wouldn't want this energetic cutie?

Charles looked down at the floor. "Oops." He pointed. "Looks like Chica had an accident."

"Oh, dear," said Mom.

Dad frowned.

When Lizzie looked down, she saw a small puddle spreading out on the floor, right where Chica stood. The black-and-white puppy squinted back at Lizzie with a mischievous expression. She almost looked pleased with herself.

See what I did? I'm a good girl, right? That's what you said when I did it before.

Uh-oh. Lizzie gulped. This could be trouble. But she wasn't about to let Charles think she was worried. "No biggie," she told everyone. "Just a mistake!" She ran to the kitchen for some paper towels and quickly cleaned up the mess. Then she took Chica outside to show her the *right* place to go — but of course Chica didn't have to go anymore. She just stood shivering on the grass until Lizzie picked her up and told her it was okay.

Half an hour later, Lizzie began to set the table for dinner. She almost didn't mind, now that she knew she would soon win the bet and have a whole month's vacation from the chore. Chica scampered around her feet as she walked back and forth from the kitchen with forks and knives, napkins and glasses. Then Lizzie saw Chica sniff and squat, right underneath the table. Fortunately, she was on the wooden floor, not on the beautiful old Oriental rug Mom had recently inherited from her great-aunt. "No, Chica." Lizzie scooped up the tiny puppy, ran her out the back door, and set her on the grass. Chica stood and squinted up at Lizzie with her head cocked to one side and her ears perfectly perked.

*It's nice out here, but why the big rush? Anyway,
now I know how to get you to take me outside to
play. All I have to do is squat down. Cool!*

Lizzie groaned. House-training a puppy could
be a real challenge. She had found that out when
the Petersons fostered their first puppy, Goldie.
But Goldie had been a quick learner. How long
would it take Chica?

Back inside, as Lizzie cleaned up Chica's latest
puddle, she reviewed the rules for house-training
in her mind. The first and most important rule:
never yell at a dog or a puppy unless you caught
her in the act. A puppy didn't understand what
she had done wrong, even if you showed her
the puddle or (Lizzie shuddered at the thought)
rubbed her nose in it.

The second rule: when the puppy did the *right*
thing, when she did her business outside, make a
big deal out of it. Give her lots and lots of praise

and petting. Eventually, once the puppy got the idea, you could start to put a word to the action. As the puppy was peeing, you could say, "Hurry up!" or "Do your business!" After a while, the puppy would learn to go on command.

It all seemed pretty straightforward, but Lizzie knew that house-training wasn't always easy. For one thing, before she could praise her puppy for going in the right place — outside — she would have to *see* Chica do it again. Lizzie had begun to think that might take a while.

"Not again." Mom came into the dining room just as Lizzie wiped up the last of the mess.

"It's not her fault," Lizzie said quickly. She did not want Mom to have any second thoughts about fostering these puppies. Even if training Chica turned out to be a bigger challenge than Lizzie had bargained for, she was determined to succeed at it. Besides, she already loved the tiny puppy. How could you not love that impish big-eyed face? "She's from a puppy mill, remember? She probably spent her first few months in a cage. She didn't have a chance to learn manners."

"Chewy did *his* business outside," Charles reported happily. He had just walked into the room, cradling the brown-and-white puppy in his arms. "Didn't you, you good boy?" He looked down at Chewy and made a kissy noise.

Lizzie knew that Charles was trying to get to her, so she smiled. "Good for him," she said. "Now all you have to work on is that chewing habit." She pointed to Chewy, who was busy chomping on Charles's shirt cuff.

Charles cleared his throat. "No problem," he said. "He's a smartie. He'll learn."

"All I ask is that you both keep a very close eye on your puppies," said Mom. "Let's keep the messes and destruction to a minimum." She looked down at the floor. "I suppose we should roll up Aunt Nell's rug for the time being and put it away."

"Totally unnecessary," Lizzie told her. "I'm on the case. I promise to watch Chica every minute."

Dad had set up a puppy crate in the kitchen, and Charles and Lizzie settled their puppies in before dinner. Chewy and Chica looked happy and cozy, cuddled together in a pile on the red flannel sheet the Petersons used for all their foster puppies.

"At least Chica won't pee in there," Lizzie said. That was one of the great things about using a puppy crate for training: dogs did not like to pee where they slept, so they would hold it while they were in the crate. (Of course, Lizzie knew it was not fair to leave a puppy in a crate for more than a couple of hours at a time, unless it was at night, when the puppy was sleeping.) After dinner, she would take Chica right outside, let her do her business, and praise her.

Dinner was lasagna left over from the night before, with salad and bread. Buddy sat right next to the Bean's chair, watching carefully for any scraps that might fall. Charles rushed through his dinner, in a hurry to get back to his puppy. Lizzie was on her second helping when she noticed that Mom had barely touched her first. Mom had not been talking much, either.

Now Mom sighed. "I just can't stop thinking about that puppy mill," she said. "What a terrible place for dogs."

"Puppy mill?" Dad asked. "I've heard about puppy mills. Is there one around here?"

Lizzie, Charles, and Mom took turns explaining where Chewy and Chica had come from.

"So this Mr. Beauregard character bought the puppies out of a truck," Dad said, "and Ms. Dobbins thinks the truck came from a puppy mill?"

"Exactly," said Mom. "And what I'm wondering

now is, did Mr. Beauregard get a license plate number for that truck?" Lizzie noticed that Mom had that certain look in her eyes — the look she got when she thought about a newspaper article she planned to write. "I'm going to call him tonight. If I can track down that truck and find the puppy mill it came from, maybe I can write an article that will help shut the place down — and maybe even change the laws about puppy mills in this state."

"Change the laws?" Dad reached for some more salad. "You're a terrific reporter, but the *Littleton News* is just a small-town paper. That sounds pretty ambitious."

"Oh, it does, does it?" asked Mom. "Okay, then, how about if *we* make a bet, too? I'll bet I can write an article that makes a difference."

"You're on." Dad stuck out his hand, and they shook on it. "And personally, I'll be hoping you can win. Those puppy mills sound like terrible places."

Lizzie agreed one hundred percent with Dad. "What's the bet for?" she asked.

Mom and Dad looked at each other and laughed. "Junk drawer," they said together. They made the same bet every time: whoever lost had to clean out the kitchen drawer that always filled up with loose change, stamps, keys to who knew what, paper clips, rubber bands, and other assorted stuff.

Lizzie laughed. Then, thinking of the kitchen reminded her of the puppy. "I'd better check on Chica." She jumped up from the table. It was probably time to take her puppy outside for a pee.

But when Lizzie reached in to take Chica out of the crate, she had a feeling that she was too late. Chica shivered slightly and squinted up at Lizzie with that impish look.

Yay! It's you! Are we headed outside again?

Lizzie patted the red flannel sheet. It was dry where Chewy lay sleeping, but sure enough, underneath Chica it was soaked. Lizzie groaned. A puppy who peed inside her crate. This was not good news. It was not good news at all.

CHAPTER FOUR

After dinner, Charles cleared the table. As he carried the dirty dishes to the kitchen, he let himself think about how great it would be to get out of that chore for a whole month. Actually, he didn't even mind the job much — but he was dying to win the bet, just to show Lizzie that she wasn't the only one who understood dogs and knew how to train them.

Could he possibly be the first one to find a great home for his puppy? He had boasted that he could, but inside he was not sure. Nobody would want to adopt a puppy who was always chewing things and chomping on body parts.

How *did* you teach a puppy not to chew? Charles realized he had to find out fast, before Chewy did some major damage. After he took Chewy outside for a pee, Charles brought his puppy upstairs to his room, where he could do some thinking.

Chewy seemed to like Charles's room. That is, he liked to *chew* it. He dashed around, sniffing and chomping everything in sight. In about five minutes, Chewy had left tiny bite marks on the leg of Charles's desk, shredded the corner of Charles's bedspread, mangled the shoe-laces on Charles's best shoes, sampled the taste of Charles's backpack straps, and nibbled on Charles's rag rug.

Charles stopped him every time, before he could do too much damage. And every time, Charles took away the thing Chewy was biting on and handed him a puppy-sized chew toy. Charles knew to do that much. You had to teach the puppy that there were some things it was *okay* to chew. But it was exhausting to have to watch Chewy's every move.

"I guess you'll sleep in a crate tonight," he told Chewy, scooping him up for the tenth time. Charles sat cross-legged on the bed with Chewy and let the puppy chomp on the cuffs of his jeans while he thought about what to do.

Sometimes, when he was trying to figure out a problem, Charles liked to sit on his bed and toss his favorite old baseball from hand to hand. There was something about the feel of the ball's worn leather and the nice plunking sound it made as it dropped into each hand. Before he knew it, ideas would start to pop into his brain. That was how he had come up with his best science fair idea yet, the one about demonstrating that ants like sweet things better than sour things. The project had involved a Tootsie Roll Pop and a pickle, and it had been the hit of that year's fair.

Charles tossed his baseball back and forth.

Sure enough, the technique worked once again.

After only about five tosses, Charles knew just what to do. Lizzie had a whole shelf of books about dog training in her room. Because of the bet, she might not lend him one if he asked. But Lizzie was downstairs, sticking close to the back door with Chica in case her puppy had to pee again. All Charles had to do was sneak in there and borrow one of the books so he could learn about how to teach puppies not to bite and chew.

It was the perfect solution. "C'mon, Chewy," he said. He picked up the puppy, marveling all over again at how light he was. When Buddy was a few weeks old, you could pick him up that easily. Not anymore. But Chewy would always be tiny, no matter how grown up he was. "How can I keep you from chewing things in Lizzie's room?" Charles asked his puppy. Chewy cocked his head and blinked his big brown eyes.

Chewing? Me?

Ha. The puppy looked so innocent, but Charles knew better. He had another brainstorm. He grabbed his backpack and helped Chewy into it. Then he zipped it up just enough that Chewy could see out but couldn't *climb* out. Chewy's adorable bug-eyed face stuck out the top. Charles kissed his puppy's nose. "That ought to do it." Charles put on the backpack and tiptoed into the hall, listening to make sure Lizzie really was downstairs. When he heard her laugh, probably at something Chica was doing, he knew the coast was clear.

Anybody who walked into Lizzie's room would know that she loved dogs. It wasn't just the shelf full of books about dogs, or the "Dog Breeds of the World" poster over her bed, or the many, many pictures of cute puppies stuck up on her bulletin board. There was also the display of miniature dog models she had started to collect, every breed from Saint Bernard to Pekingese. And the stuffed dogs on her bed. And the dog magazines on her nightstand. Lizzie's room was All Dogs, All the Time.

Charles put his backpack down on the floor and made sure that Chewy could still see out. Then he knelt by the bookcase and scanned the titles: *Best Dog Tricks Ever. How to Be Your Dog's Best Friend. The Complete Idiot's Guide to Owning a Dog.*

None of the books seemed quite right. Charles did not want to teach Chewy tricks — at least, not until after he had taught him to stop chewing. As for being his puppy's best friend, that was easy. Who needed a book for that? And even though Charles was not sure how to teach Chewy not to chew, he would not call himself a complete idiot.

Then he spotted the perfect book: *Top 10 Puppy Problems and How to Solve Them*, by Mickey Milligan. He knew that name. Wasn't that the dog trainer with long blond hair, the one who was always on TV and in magazines? Charles pulled out the book and flipped through it to look for Chewy's problem. "Ah, here it is. Chewing and biting." He snapped the book shut. "This is it, Chewy." He smiled over at his backpack — but Chewy's head wasn't sticking out anymore. "Chewy?" Charles went over and opened the backpack. The puppy must have squirmed his way out. "Chewy!" Charles looked wildly around the room, hoping against hope that Chewy had not destroyed some precious belonging of Lizzie's.

He did not see the brown-and-white puppy anywhere.

Charles grabbed the book and ran back down the hall to his room. "Chewy!" he cried. The good news was that Chewy was right there in Charles's room. The tiny pup blinked up at Charles with those big brown eyes. The bad news? Chewy lay on Charles's bed, gnawing his favorite baseball to shreds.

CHAPTER FIVE

of Lizzie. But Chica was really fast. Charles sat up. The flashlight lit up Dr. Gibson with her . . . The string . . . the end of the tail . . . Lizzie . . . Charles . . . . to breath.

Lizzie noticed the missing book the second she walked into her room. At first she was mad. For one thing, Charles wasn't supposed to be in her room without permission. For another, he should not have taken her book without asking. But then she decided to let it go. She practically knew that Mickey Milligan book by heart already, anyway. In fact, she remembered with a sinking sensation, didn't he say that some small dogs could be almost impossible to house-train? Oh, well. What did Mickey Milligan know?

Lizzie looked under "house-training" in some of her other dog-training books. Then she sat on her bed, with Chica cradled in her lap, and thought.

The whole idea with house-training was to, as one book said, "set your puppy up for success, not failure." In other words, make sure the puppy had lots of chances to do her business in the right place and do your best never, ever to let her go in the wrong place. That meant taking the puppy outside after every meal and play session (since sometimes the excitement of playing makes puppies have to go), before bed, and right after waking up — at the very least.

Could Chica get through the night without making a mistake? Lizzie did not think so. She carried her puppy down the hall to Mom's study. "Mom?" she asked. "Since it's vacation week, is it okay if I set my alarm for midnight so I can get up with Chica and take her outside?"

"I think that would be all right," Mom said. She smiled at Lizzie. "Guess what? I got Mr. Beauregard's phone number from Ms. Dobbins. I called and asked him if he remembered that truck's license plate. He didn't, exactly. But I think he gave me enough letters and numbers to start a search. I've already passed them along to my friend at the police station."

"That's great, Mom!" Lizzie moved Chica's tiny paws to make it look as if the puppy were clapping. "Chica says, 'Yay!'"

After she had taken her puppy outside one last time, Lizzie brought Chica down to Charles's room so she could see that her brother, Chewy, would be sleeping right next door. The two puppies touched noses and wagged tails, but neither of them cried when Lizzie picked Chica up to take her away. That was good news. The puppies already felt secure in their new place.

Back in her room, Lizzie tucked Chica into the crate Dad had brought upstairs. The pup must have been very tired out from her long day. She curled right up, tiny nose to tiny tail, and went to sleep.

Lizzie got up with the puppy four times that night. Each time, she stumbled downstairs with

Chica in her arms and went out the back door with the puppy, holding a flashlight so that she could see whether Chica peed in the yard. Sometimes she did, and Lizzie made a big fuss over her and told her what a good girl she was. And sometimes she didn't. Either way, when Lizzie fell back into bed each time, she reset her alarm so Chica would have another chance in two hours.

When Lizzie woke up for good the next morning, she felt bleary-eyed and exhausted. She peeked inside the crate. Chica squinted back at her with that mischievous expression. She shivered a bit, too.

Oh, no, thought Lizzie. But when she touched the blanket beneath Chica, it was dry. Success! The puppy must have been shivering with excitement because she had made it through the night. Lizzie took Chica out of the crate and covered her with kisses. Then she ran the puppy downstairs and straight outside. When

Chica squatted and peed, Lizzie swooped her up and kissed her all over again. "What a good puppy."

Chica trembled with happiness.

Gee, this person sure does like to make a fuss over nothing! Oh, well. I love the attention.

Lizzie went back inside and set the kitchen timer for twenty minutes. When it dinged, she took Chica out again. She did that all morning long, taking Chica outside whenever the timer dinged, no matter what she was doing when it went off. Lizzie figured that if she brought Chica outside before even *Chica* knew she had to pee, maybe the puppy would do the right thing more often.

Mom was impressed. "You're really taking your job seriously, Lizzie," she said.

"It's my new training plan," Lizzie told her. "I

call it the Twenty-Minute Plan. It came to me in the middle of the night. If it works, I'll make a million dollars and be as famous as Mickey Milligan."

"That's great, Lizzie. And we have another young dog trainer in the house. Have you noticed?" She nodded at the Bean, who tugged on Buddy's leash as he took the puppy outside. "Every time you go out, he takes Buddy out. I make him wait until you're done so the puppies each have their space. It's wonderful. Buddy gets plenty of attention and exercise, and the Bean stays busy. Maybe I'll even be able to get some work done on my article."

Later that morning, Lizzie's friend Maria called. "I am so tired," Maria said, yawning into the phone. "I hardly got any sleep at all last night."

"Neither did I." Lizzie yawned, too. Why were yawns so catching? She told Maria about her

55

night with Chica. "I was up at two A.M., four A.M., and six A.M." She explained the Twenty-Minute Plan to Maria. "So, why didn't *you* sleep?"

"I couldn't stop thinking about that puppy mill and how horrible it must be," said Maria. "Those poor puppies. I want to do something nice for the ones Ms. Dobbins has at the shelter. Dad said he'd drive me to that new PetLove store so I can buy them some special treats. Want to come?"

"Definitely." Then Lizzie spotted the timer and remembered. "Oops. What am I thinking? I can't go. I have to watch Chica."

"Maybe Charles would take her out a few times," suggested Maria.

"I doubt it. He's busy with Chewy, and besides, we're kind of at war." She told Maria about the bet. "He wants to win as much as I do. Why would he help me train my puppy?"

Mom waved a hand at Lizzie. "Do you need some help?" she asked. "I can keep an eye on

Chica while I work at my desk. You've been very responsible. You deserve a break."

"Really? Thanks, Mom." Lizzie spoke into the phone again. "I can go!"

"Pick you up in ten minutes," said Maria.

Lizzie used the time to make sure Mom understood the Twenty-Minute Plan. She explained how to praise Chica if the puppy happened to pee while she was outside, and how to watch for signs that she might need to go, like sniffing the floor, circling, or squatting.

At the shopping center, Maria and Lizzie headed into PetLove while Maria's dad stopped in to say hello to his friend Manny, who owned Rispoli's Hardware next door. PetLove was a huge store, with everything you could possibly need for pets stacked from floor to ceiling in long aisles. Pet beds, pet dishes, pet food. Hamster habitats, fish tanks, birdcages. There was even a whole section dedicated to nothing but snakes and lizards.

Lizzie usually loved pet stores, but this one was almost too big, with too much to look at. After they wandered up and down a few aisles in a daze, she and Maria finally found their way to aisle twelve (cat and dog treats) and picked out an assortment of goodies for the puppies. Then they headed for aisle ten (dog toys) and added a squeaky hamburger, a rubber carrot, and a stuffed purple-and-green dinosaur to their basket. Ms. Dobbins was always glad to accept donations of new toys for her shelter dogs and puppies.

Then, when they were on their way to the checkout counter, Lizzie spotted the cages. Three forlorn dachshund puppies stared back at her from one cage, and in another, a skinny black Lab hung back in a corner while her brothers and sisters slept in a pile. A frantic terrier pawed at his cage, scrabbling as if he thought he could break free. One glance made Lizzie want to cry.

She wished she were as rich as Mr. Beauregard so she could buy them all and take them home to love. "Wait! Look!" She tugged on Maria's shirt. "They sell puppies here."

"Wow," said Maria. "They're adorable. Let's stop and say hello to them."

Lizzie pulled her friend away. "Ms. Dobbins said that sometimes these big pet stores get their puppies from puppy mills," she whispered.

"What?" Maria's face turned white.

"Look at those puppies. Do they look healthy?" Lizzie grabbed Maria's arm. "Come on, let's go find out where those puppies come from." She marched up to the counter.

The girl at the cash register shrugged. "I don't know," she said. "Ask him. He's one of the managers." She pointed to a skinny guy with glasses by the front door. Like her, he wore a red T-shirt with "PetLove. We Love Your Pets!" embroidered on the chest pocket.

"Lizzie," Maria said, "are you sure —" Maria didn't always like it when Lizzie spoke her mind about things or made a scene.

But Lizzie had already headed for the manager. "Excuse me, sir?" She tapped the skinny guy on the arm. "Can you tell me where those puppies came from?"

"Puppies aren't exactly my department." The manager shrugged. "You'd have to talk to Mr. Sneed, the owner of this store. But I'm pretty sure they come from a breeder around here some-where. The guy who delivers them drives a truck. White, with red stripes."

Lizzie took the basket of treats and toys from Maria and set it down on the floor. "That's all I needed to know," she said. "Come on, Maria. We're not buying anything at *this* store." And with that, she marched out the door.

Maria's dad met them out front. "Not one puppy biscuit in that whole giant store?" he asked when they got into the car empty-handed.

Lizzie was too mad to answer, but Maria explained. "They sell puppies in there," she told her dad. "Puppies from that puppy mill I told you about."

"That's awful." Mr. Santiago frowned. "How can they call themselves PetLove if they do something like that?" He started the car. "I can't imagine that any responsible pet owner would want to shop there if they knew."

Maria's dad drove them to the supermarket to buy puppy treats. "These aren't so special," said Maria, "but they'll do." When they arrived at Caring Paws, Lizzie spotted Mr. Beauregard's big black car parked outside the shelter. Inside, everyone was busy taking care of the new puppies. Andrew cleaned kennels while Julie walked three pups at once. In the grooming area, Ms. Dobbins and Mr. Beauregard were giving puppy baths. Mr. Beauregard whooped and laughed as he soaped up a black Lab. "This is more fun than wrasslin' alligators!" he told Lizzie and Maria.

Ms. Dobbins looked tired, but she smiled, too. "Mr. Beauregard has been a huge help. He's skipping a meeting about a million-dollar deal, just to be here!" she said, wiping some suds off her nose.

Lizzie told Ms. Dobbins about the puppies for sale at PetLove.

"Shops like PetLove keep the puppy mills in business." Ms. Dobbins sighed. "They need lots of puppies to sell, so the puppy mills keep supplying more. Meanwhile, there are already plenty of puppies in shelters like this one, just waiting to be adopted."

"Why can't pet stores just have *shelter* puppies for people to adopt?" Lizzie asked.

"Some do," Ms. Dobbins said. "I work with some other pet stores around here. They feature puppies, dogs, cats, and kittens from our shelter. They have a sign that explains where the animals came from, and they charge just a little more than we charge here as an adoption fee. They make some money, and pass the rest along to us to help cover any care we've given the animals, like shots or flea baths."

"So why can't PetLove do that?" Lizzie demanded.

"I've already asked." Ms. Dobbins shook her head. "As soon as they announced plans to open, I spoke to the owner, Mr. Sneed, and offered to work with them. But he thought it would be too much trouble."

"Trouble?" Lizzie clenched her fists. "How can he run a pet store if he doesn't even care about dogs?"

"Makes you madder than a hornet, doesn't it?" asked Mr. Beauregard. "My advice is, take that anger and try to *do* something with it. That's why I'm here washing these pups. Better than walking around feelin' steamed about that puppy mill place."

Lizzie nodded. That was probably good advice — but what could she do to change Mr. Sneed's mind?

CHAPTER SIX

"Grrr," growled Charles. "Yip-yip-yip!"

Chewy looked up at Charles in surprise.

What? You mean that hurts?

The puppy stopped chomping on Charles's thumb.

"It works!" Charles said. He kissed Chewy on the top of his apple-shaped head. "Good boy." He grinned at Sammy. Charles and his friend were in the backyard, playing with Chewy — and training the puppy with a brand-new method, Charles's idea.

Chewy licked Charles's chin. Then the licking

turned into nibbling. Then the nibbling turned into biting.

"Yip!" said Charles. "Grrr — yip!"

Chewy stopped biting and blinked up at Charles.

You don't like that? Oh, okay, then I won't do it.

"Good boy," Charles said again. He rummaged in his pocket for a puppy treat. "Here you go." Charles smiled down at the tiny puppy in his arms. "You're learning," he said. "You really are."

"What is going *on* out here?" The back door slammed and Lizzie appeared on the deck with Chica in her arms. She stomped down the stairs and put her puppy on the grass. Chica scampered right over to where Charles, Sammy, and Chewy sat.

Hey, bro! I've missed you!

Chewy sprang out of Charles's arms and tumbled over his own feet in his hurry to meet his sister.

Yay! It's you!

Chica jumped on top of Chewy. Chewy wriggled out from underneath his sister and put a paw across her back while he chomped on her ear. Chica squealed and batted Chewy away, then charged over to jump on top of him and bite his tail. Chewy yipped and rolled over, pawing madly at Chica's face. The puppies rolled and tumbled and chased each other around the yard in a blur of black- and brown-and-white. Chewy stopped near a pink rosebush to pee, and Chica did, too. Then they started to dash around again.

Charles laughed so hard his stomach hurt. Sammy laughed, too. But Lizzie barely cracked a smile. "Why are you two out here barking at Chewy?" she asked.

"We're trying to teach him not to bite people," Charles said. "It's my new training idea, and it's working." Charles was proud of his idea, because he had come up with it all by himself. Well, mostly. Mickey Milligan had helped. "See, I read in this, uh, book that puppies learn not to bite from playing with their brothers and sisters. You know, like these two were just doing. Did you see how Chica squealed when Chewy bit her? That's how puppies learn that biting hurts. Mother dogs teach their puppies, too, by growling at them when they bite too hard."

"Okay," said Lizzie. "I'm with you so far. Chewy needs to understand that it hurts when he bites. But why don't you just tell him, 'No!'?"

"I hate to yell at him," Charles said. "He's so sensitive. If I yell, he'll just tremble and look up at me with those big, bulgy eyes of his. I can't take it. I decided that instead of yelling, I would just act like I was Chewy's puppy brother," Charles said. "Chewy has to understand that

67

biting hurts people, just like it hurts other puppies. If I don't say anything, he doesn't know. But if Sammy or I bark or squeal, he stops right away — at least for a second. That gives me time to praise him for *not* chewing. It really works."

"That," said Lizzie, "is the weirdest dog-training idea I ever heard. But hey, good luck with it. You'll still never win our bet, because I'm way ahead of you. My Twenty-Minute Plan works so well that Chica hasn't had an accident all day. Tomorrow we'll go to the Thirty-Minute Plan. Chica's almost ready for a forever home, and I'll find her one soon."

"Chewy's almost ready, too," said Charles. "The contest isn't over yet, you know."

Lizzie sighed and plopped down on the ground next to Charles. She plucked a piece of grass from the lawn and started to shred it. "Even if we do find homes for Chewy and Chica, that's only two puppies. Then there are all the puppies at the shelter — they need homes, too — and the puppy mills just keep turning out *more* puppies to sell to stores like PetLove." She told Charles and Sammy about the puppies at the store, and how she and Maria had decided not to buy anything there, and how Ms. Dobbins had already asked Mr. Sneed not to sell puppy mill puppies but he had refused. "It just made me so mad."

"So let's do something about it," said Charles.

"That's what Mr. Beauregard said. But what can we do?" asked Lizzie.

Charles thought for a moment. "What about a petition?"

Charles liked the idea of petitions. He had recently helped his mom take one around the neighborhood. The petition was a piece of paper with an explanation at the top about why the town needed a new soccer field. Charles and his mom convinced a lot of people to sign their names to say they agreed. Other people were taking petitions around their neighborhoods, too. When they had enough signatures, they would show the petition to the people in charge at the town government, and say, "Look! Five hundred people signed this petition that says we should have a new soccer field." Then the town would have to do something about it. Charles's favorite part of the petition was at the top, where big old-fashioned letters said *WE, THE UNDERSIGNED* . . . He thought that sounded cool and important, like a phrase right out of history. "We could get people to sign a petition against puppy mills."

"Not a bad idea." Lizzie nodded slowly. "But we need more. We need something dramatic, something that'll make people think twice before they shop at PetLove." She plucked three more blades of grass and began to braid them.

By now, Chica had settled on her lap, and Chewy was on Charles's. Chewy was snuggled up, all cozy, and not biting for once. Charles patted him softly. It was great to have a dog that could curl up right in your lap. Buddy was already getting too big for that. These Chihuahuas sure did love to be close to their people. Charles thought that if he ever had one for keeps, he would want to slip him into his pocket and take him everywhere.

"I just know that if other people understood how bad puppy mills are, they wouldn't want to shop at PetLove any more than I do." Lizzie threw down her half-made braid. "I've got it!" she said suddenly. "A protest. Like, a demonstration. We can march around with signs in front of PetLove, and let people know why they shouldn't shop there. We'll get all the dog lovers we know to come out, with their dogs. That will definitely attract attention."

Charles had to admit that it was a great idea. "It could be our first real Caring Club activity," he said, "because we'll be educating people. And maybe it will even make that Mr. Sneed think again about selling puppies who come from puppy mills."

Sammy wanted to run home for cardboard and

paints so they could start making signs right away. But just then, the Bean came out onto the deck, holding Buddy's leash. "Uppies!" he yelled. As soon as he started down the stairs, Chewy and Chica began to yip and yap. Buddy took one look at the Chihuahuas and towed the Bean across the yard in the opposite direction. Charles and Lizzie grabbed the Chihuahuas' collars. Buddy deserved to be out in his own backyard without being chased.

Buddy stood in one corner of the yard and barked at the Chihuahuas. Chewy and Chica yipped back at him. Even Rufus and Goldie, in their own yard next door at Sammy's house, began to bark.

Charles and Sammy looked at each other and shrugged. Then they began to yip and bark, too. A second later, Lizzie and the Bean joined in with their own barking. Charles laughed as he yipped. He wasn't even sure why they had all started to bark together, but it sure was fun. He felt like they were all just one big pack of dogs.

"Hey! What's all the racket?" Dad came out the back door and glared at them, hands on his hips. "Quiet down out here, all you dogs. Your mom's trying to get some work done upstairs." He went over to help the Bean control Buddy.

Slowly, the barking petered out. "That's better," said Dad. "Now, whose turn is it to set the table? It's almost dinnertime."

For a few moments, between planning the demonstration and barking together, Charles had been having such a good time that he'd forgotten all about the bet. He could tell that Lizzie had forgotten, too. But at the words "set the table," it all came back. It was great to bark together, but he had to remember: this was war.

Sammy nudged Charles. Charles knew what that meant. "Can Sammy eat over?" he asked.

Dad smiled. Charles knew what *that* meant, too. Dad joked sometimes that Sammy ate more meals at the Petersons' than at his own house. "Sure, there's plenty for everyone."

Charles picked Chewy up. "Come on, Sammy. It's my turn, so if you want to stay, you have to help me set the table."

"Hope you like that job, because soon it'll be your turn for a whole month," Lizzie teased. "Once I win that bet."

Charles made a face at Lizzie as he and Sammy went inside. The war was definitely back on. "She thinks she's so smart," Charles muttered, gathering forks, knives, and napkins. Sammy filled water glasses at the kitchen sink and carried them to the table, spilling only a little here and there along the way.

"Hey, want to teach Lizzie a lesson?" Sammy asked as he placed the glasses on the table. "I just thought of the best idea."

Charles put down the last fork and knife, at his dad's place. He looked at Sammy. Sammy had a lot of ideas. Not all of them worked out so well, but they were almost always fun in the beginning. "What did you have in mind?"

CHAPTER SEVEN

Charles put down the just Pack and Kate at his desk place. He looked at Sammy who had a lot of drawings on it. He knew maybe just as well but thought it could what maybe into this begin... ... ...

Ding. Upstairs, Lizzie's timer went off. She jumped up from the computer, where she was busy downloading information about puppy mills. She looked at the tiny puppy who sat alertly by her feet. "Come on, Chica. Time to go out." Chica squinted back at her and let out a happy yip.

Again? Already? Well, okay! Fine with me. I'll go anywhere with you.

Lizzie scooped up the tiny pup and headed downstairs. Charles and Sammy had finished setting the table, but dinner wasn't quite ready yet. Good. She had so much to do to prepare for the big demonstration. She had already been on the phone with Maria, talking about it. They had decided on Friday, the day after next, as the perfect day. Lizzie had already printed out some informational brochures about why puppy mills should be banned. She could hardly stand to look at the pictures of skinny puppies all crowded into tiny cages. She'd saved one to give to Mom, for research for her article, and left one on Charles's bed. He could use the facts in it when he wrote up his petition.

Lizzie heard Charles and Sammy whisper and giggle in the living room as she walked by. What were those two up to now? How many times had Sammy come up with some wild idea — and then talked Charles into doing something crazy? If you asked Lizzie, she'd say Sammy was a bad influence. He was funny, though; she had to admit that. Sammy always had a joke ready.

Outside, Lizzie put Chica down on the grass. The puppy scampered right over to the rosebush where Chewy and she had peed earlier. She squatted and peed. Then she cocked her head and squinted at Lizzie.

I bet this is why you brought me out here. Am I right? Am I right? Am I right?

"Good girl." Lizzie ran over and scooped her up. "Oh, Chica, you're really learning, aren't you? What a good girl." She kissed Chica's nose, and the top of her head, and each of her ears. Chica trembled — and this time Lizzie could tell it was from happiness.

Back inside, Chica let out a yip.

Hey, bro! Where are you?

Chewy yipped back from the living room.

In here! Come find me!

Chica ran to find her brother. "Okay, Chica, you go play," said Lizzie. She set her timer again and carried it upstairs, reminding herself to write up a description of her Twenty-Minute Plan to post on her favorite dog-training chat group. The plan really was a success. Soon she'd be taking Chica out every half hour, then every hour — until, in a few days, she wouldn't need the timer at all anymore. By then, Chica would definitely be ready for a forever home.

Upstairs, Lizzie knocked on the door of her mom's study. Mom was on the phone. She held up a hand to tell Lizzie to wait a second. Buddy and the Bean lay next to Mom's desk, curled up together on Buddy's dog bed. Sometimes the Bean liked to pretend he was a puppy.

"Thank you, Senator. I look forward to meeting with you." Mom finished her phone call and hung up. She threw her hands into the air. "Yes! That's terrific. Senator Bisbee is willing to meet with me to hear more about puppy mills and why our state should make them illegal."

"Mom, that's so great." Lizzie gave her mom a high five. Then she thought of something. She was so excited that she started to jump up and down. Buddy got excited, too. He scrambled up from his bed and spun around in circles. The Bean copied him, pretending to chase his own invisible tail.

"Mom, Mom, Mom, you have to call the senator back!" Lizzie said. "Tell him to come to our demonstration. He'll learn everything he needs to know about puppy mills."

Mom looked puzzled. "Demonstration?"

"Yes! It's our first official Caring Club activity." Lizzie explained it all: about PetLove's buying puppies from puppy mills, about the plan she and Charles and Sammy had come up with, even about the idea Maria had added — that they should advertise a free dog wash so that lots of pet owners would be sure to come by. Maria's dad was going to ask his friend Manny if they could set up the dog wash outside his hardware store.

"Well," said Mom. "You certainly have been busy. What does Ms. Dobbins think of all this?"

"She loves the idea," said Lizzie. "She told me all the best websites to go to for information about puppy mills. Probably some of the same ones you've checked out for your article. Have you seen the one with pictures of —"

"Lizzie!" Charles yelled from downstairs. "You better get down here."

"Uh-oh," said Lizzie. Without even finishing her sentence, she dashed out of her mom's office and down the stairs. "What is it?" she asked. "Where's Chica?"

Charles led her into the hallway and pointed to a puddle on the floor. "I guess Chica couldn't wait twenty minutes this time."

"Oh, no." Lizzie looked at Chica, who sat under the phone table in the hall. The puppy squinted back, trembling all over and wagging her tail hopefully.

Who, me?

"Oh, Chica," sighed Lizzie. But she didn't yell or even say, "No." It was too late for that. The deed was done — and it was probably her own fault, anyway. Maybe she should have let Chica stay outside longer last time, instead of rushing right back upstairs. She picked the puppy up and ran to the back door. Even though it was too late, Lizzie knew that it was good to show her where she *should* have gone.

She set Chica on the grass near the rosebush. The puppy sat there and looked at Lizzie, her head tilted quizzically. Lizzie thought she looked upset. "Don't worry about it, Chica." She picked her up and scratched between her ears. Chica loved that. "It wasn't your fault." Chica wriggled happily.

Me, worry? What do I have to worry about?

Back inside, Lizzie cleaned up the puddle with paper towels while Sammy and Charles watched. "Too bad." Charles shook his head. "Just when she was doing so well, too."

Sammy clucked his tongue. "I guess Mickey Milligan doesn't have to worry about the competition from that Twenty-Minute Plan of yours."

Lizzie gritted her teeth. "Maybe *you* should worry about minding your own business," she said. "Anyway, that was just one small mistake. It doesn't mean a thing. We won't let it happen again, will we, Chica?" She scooped her up and cuddled the tiny pup next to her face. Chica trembled, then licked Lizzie's cheek. Lizzie carried Chica back upstairs with her head held high, trying to ignore the whispers and giggles from her annoying brother and his pesty friend. What did *they* know about dog training?

Downstairs, Sammy and Charles giggled so hard they could barely manage to smack each other a high five. "That was so awesome!" Sammy gasped.

Charles thought of the look on Lizzie's face when she first saw the puddle. Ha. Miss Know-It-All sure had gotten a surprise, hadn't she? "Awesome," he agreed.

"How long do you think we have to wait until we do it again?" Sammy asked when he finally caught his breath.

"Again?" Charles wasn't sure about that.

"Definitely," Sammy said. "Come on! It was hilarious."

Upstairs, Lizzie reset her timer and carried it and Chica back to Mom's study.

"Everything okay?" Mom asked.

"Fine," said Lizzie. "Just a tiny setback. No problem. It's all cleaned up. So, will you call him? Please?"

"Lizzie," Mom said, "I get it that you want me to call Senator Bisbee. And I will. But I have a lot of other research and writing to do on this article, so it might not happen tonight. Anyway, it's nearly dinnertime and I don't want to bother him." She spun around on her chair and looked straight at Lizzie. "But guess what? I just heard from my friend at the police station. I asked him to try to trace the numbers Mr. Beauregard gave me. You know, from the license plate of that truck that sells the puppies."

"And?" Lizzie held her breath.

"He turned up a truck registered to a company name. Pretty Pups, Incorporated."

Lizzie felt her heart start to pound. "So it *is* a puppy mill."

"Probably." Mom nodded. "I'll find out for sure tomorrow. Sammy's dad and I are heading out there. We'll pose as a couple looking for a dog, but really I'll be gathering facts for a story and he'll be trying to get some pictures."

Sammy's dad was a photographer who sometimes took pictures for the *Littleton News*. "Mom! Really? Can I come with you?"

"No, Lizzie." Mom spoke gently, but she looked very serious. "I don't think you'd want to be there. From what I have read about puppy mills, it won't be a very pretty sight."

Lizzie nodded. She remembered some of the puppy mill pictures she had seen online. Skinny, sick-looking puppies of every size and shape, packed into dark, dirty cages with hardly enough space to turn around. In the pictures, their sad eyes stared out from the cages as if pleading, "Save me, save me!" Lizzie had already had one bad dream about Buddy being trapped in a cage like that. Seeing the real thing would probably give her a lifetime's worth of nightmares. "I guess you're right. But I can't wait to read the story you write."

"Well, who knows for sure if there even *is* a story?" Mom asked. "We'll find out tomorrow and take it from there."

Lizzie heard Charles and Sammy come upstairs. Again they whispered and giggled. What *were* those two up to? Then Chewy let out a "yip-yip-yip," and Chica leapt off Lizzie's lap and scampered down the hall to find her brother.

"Okay, Mom," said Lizzie. "But tomorrow, before you go out to the puppy mill, will you —"

"Yes, I promise. I'll call the senator and tell him about your demonstration."

"Thanks, Mom," said Lizzie. She got up and went to find Chica. But on her way to Charles's room, Lizzie saw something that made her gasp.

A puddle.

Just a small one.

In the middle of the hall.

How could it be possible? The timer had not even gone off again yet, and Chica had just peed in the *downstairs* hall. Lizzie marched down to Charles's room and walked in without knocking. Sammy and Charles were on the floor, playing with the puppies. Charles looked up at her with an expression just like Chewy's: all wide-eyed innocence. "Hi, Lizzie," he said. "What's up?"

Lizzie did not want to give him the satisfaction of knowing that Chica had made another mistake. So without a word, she just scooped up her naughty puppy and swept her out of the room, down the stairs, and out the door. She set Chica down by the rosebush and watched as the puppy sniffed around for a moment. Then Chica sat back and looked up at Lizzie. She tilted her head.

Now what did I do?

"Poor Chica," Lizzie said. "You must be confused, or upset or something. Was it because of the way I stomped around all afternoon, when I was mad about the puppies at PetLove? Was that it? Maybe you're really sensitive. Maybe that's it." Lizzie felt awful. Whatever it was, she was sure it was her fault that Chica was making all these mistakes. The great dog trainer. Ha. Maybe Chica was more of a challenge than she could handle.

Lizzie sighed and headed back toward the house. "C'mon, Chica. It must be almost time for dinner."

Upstairs, Sammy and Charles had watched the whole thing from the window. Sammy laughed, but Charles had started to feel sorry for Lizzie, not to mention Chica. The poor puppy was probably totally confused by now. "Maybe we should tell her," he suggested.

"No way!" Sammy's eyes were bright. "Not yet. One more time. Come on, Cheese. Don't chicken out on me now."

Charles hesitated. Had Lizzie learned her lesson? Would she quit being such a know-it-all? Was she ready to stop acting so sure that she would win the bet? Hmm. Maybe not quite yet. "Okay," he said. "But just one more time."

"Dinnertime," Dad called from the kitchen.

Charles gathered his tiny dog into his arms. "Let's go, Chewy." The puppy mouthed his hand, but before Charles could even squeak, Chewy eased up and stopped biting. "Good boy." Charles carried Chewy downstairs. In the dining room, Lizzie had just set a big platter of asparagus on the table. Chica trotted along by her feet.

Charles put Chewy down and Chica dashed over to say hello. Tails wagging, the two puppies touched noses and trembled happily, as if they hadn't seen each other for days instead of minutes.

When Lizzie headed back into the kitchen to bring out more food, Sammy elbowed Charles. "Now!" he whispered.

Charles glanced around to make sure nobody could see what he was about to do. Then he pulled a small bottle out of his pocket and poured a puddle of water onto the floor. He was careful to get as close as he could to a corner of Mom's beautiful old rug without actually wetting it.

CHAPTER EIGHT

Charles held his breath. His heart pounded. Any minute now, somebody would come in and see the puddle. He wished he had never started this whole business. Why had he let Sammy talk him into it?

He was just about to grab a napkin from the table and mop up the puddle when the Bean and Mom walked into the dining room. "I shut Buddy up," the Bean announced proudly.

"Shut him up?" asked Charles. "I didn't hear him barking again."

"He means he shut Buddy up in his room while we have dinner," Mom explained. "He's seen you do that when we have to temporarily keep Buddy away from our other foster pups. What a smartie."

She patted the Bean's head. But the Bean wasn't paying attention anymore. He'd spotted something.

"Puppy uh-oh!" He pointed to the puddle on the floor.

Charles looked down. He was horrified to see that the puddle had seeped into the corner of the rug, creating a large, round, dark stain.

"What's that, sweetie?" Mom asked the Bean. Then she looked down, too. "Aaah! My rug! These puppies are out of control."

"It wasn't Chewy," Sammy said quickly. "I was holding him." Sure enough, he had the brown-and-white pup snuggled in his arms.

"Chica?" Lizzie came back into the room with a bowl of potatoes. Her face fell when she saw the puddle. "Oh, Chica, you didn't."

Chica sat near the puddle. She squinted up at Lizzie and trembled all over.

No, I didn't! I really, really didn't!

Lizzie scooped up the pup and ran her to the back door.

Dad poked his head into the dining room. "What's going on?" he asked.

Mom just pointed to the puddle on the floor. "Oh, no," said Dad. "That's no good. I wondered if caring for two puppies would be too much."

Sammy nudged Charles and smiled, but Charles didn't smile back. He didn't feel much like smiling anymore. Lizzie was really upset. Mom was mad. Dad was probably about to say that they couldn't keep the puppies. And poor Chica probably thought she had done something terrible.

"It's not what you think," Charles burst out. He reached into his pocket and pulled out the little bottle just as Lizzie returned with Chica and a handful of paper towels. "It's only water."

"Charles!" said Dad. "You mean you poured water on the floor and let Lizzie believe it was Chica making a mistake?"

Charles looked down at his feet. "I'm sorry," he said. "I'm really sorry." He held up his hands. "It was just supposed to be kind of a joke."

"Well, it wasn't very funny." Mom frowned at Charles. "Honestly, Charles. I thought that puppy had ruined my rug."

"That's not like you, Charles." Dad shook his head.

Charles felt his face grow hot. Dad was right. It *wasn't* like him. "It was kind of funny the first time," he said, trying to explain. "Then — I don't know. We just kept doing it."

Lizzie glared at Charles. "I don't believe it. You mean every one of those puddles tonight was just *water*?" She shoved the paper towels at him. "You are really something else. And guess what? You can forget about your stupid petition idea. You are hereby *un*invited to our demonstration."

"But —" Charles saw the way Mom and Dad were looking at him, and he decided it might be better not to say another word. He could try blaming Sammy — but he knew it wasn't really his friend's fault. After all, he had agreed to the idea. So he just said, "I'm sorry," again as he squatted down to clean up the water. He wished he could scuttle under the table and thump his tail while he peeked out pleadingly, the way Buddy did when he knew he'd done something wrong. Lizzie always forgave Buddy. Maybe she would forgive him, too.

Sammy cleared his throat. "Um, you know what? I think I'll go home for dinner after all." He handed Chewy to Charles and slipped away, leaving Charles to sit through a very quiet family dinner.

For the rest of the evening, Charles thought about how he could make it up to Lizzie. He tossed his shredded baseball from hand to hand, but no ideas popped into his brain. Maybe the magic was gone now that the baseball was ruined. He flopped around in bed all night as he tried to come up with an idea. Finally, when the first light of morning brightened his windows and he heard a robin singing outside, Charles jumped out of bed. After he took Chewy out, he went to his closet and rummaged around until he found an old pad of newsprint he used to draw on. He brought it to his desk. Then, at the top, he lettered very carefully *WE, THE UNDERSIGNED . . .*

He had to wait until nine in the morning to call Sammy — that was the rule — but at 9:01 he dialed. "Sammy," he said when his friend answered. "I need your help. And you know you owe me one."

Mom had left the house early, heading out with Sammy's dad to investigate the puppy mill. She hoped to finish her article and turn it in that day so it could come out on the morning of the demonstration. But Charles's dad was happy to drive Charles and Sammy downtown. They brought along Chewy and Sammy's dogs, Rufus and

Goldie, and set up a table in front of Lucky Dog Books, the bookstore owned by their friend Jerry Small. Charles set out his petition and the brochure Lizzie had printed out. Then Jerry helped him and Sammy hang up the huge sign Charles had made that morning using every color of marker he owned. It said

CALLING ALL ANIMAL LOVERS!
DEMONSTRATE AGAINST PUPPY MILLS
TOMORROW FROM 10:00 TO 12:00!
DOG WASH TO BENEFIT CARING PAWS ONLY $2!

Charles had cut out pictures of puppies and dogs from a magazine and pasted them all over the sign, and he'd drawn a border of paw prints. It looked pretty good.

"That'll definitely attract some attention," Jerry said. He stroked his chin. "But I wonder if you should add a few words about *where* the demonstration will be."

Oops. Charles grabbed a thick black marker he'd brought (just in case) and wrote *AT PETLOVE STORE* in big block letters, squeezed in around the rest.

"What's this all about?" A woman approached the table. Maybe she would be the first to sign the petition. She read out loud: "'We, the under-signed, believe that puppy mills should be illegal in our state. There are enough unwanted puppies in the world without the puppy mills making more of them. Send a message to our lawmakers! Ban the puppy mills! Also, tell PetLove not to sell puppies from puppy mills.'" She turned away from the petition and picked up a brochure, say-ing, "Hmm," and "Oh, dear," as she read. "That's just awful," she said finally. She put down the brochure and looked one more time at the empty petition. Then she walked away.

"Hey," said Charles. But she didn't turn around.

Jerry Small went over to the petition.

"Sometimes it helps if there's already another signature on there." He signed his name with a flourish.

Charles and Sammy signed beneath Jerry's name. Now the petition looked much, much better. Charles just knew that the next person who looked at it would sign it.

Back at home, Lizzie and Maria were in the kitchen, surrounded by bowls and spoons and bags of ingredients. Every inch of the kitchen — the counters, the handle of the fridge, the sink, and both girls — was covered with a fine dusting of flour. "This was a great idea." Lizzie wiped some flour off her nose. "Why buy dog biscuits from PetLove when we can make our own to give away at the demonstration?" She began to measure out a tablespoon of brewer's yeast when her timer went off with a ding. "Oops. Time to go out, Chica." She picked up the pup and whisked her outside.

Chica trotted right over to the rosebush and did her business.

I get it! I definitely get it! This is what you want me to do when we come out here!

"I am still so mad at Charles," Lizzie said to Maria after she'd praised Chica and brought her inside. "How could he pull such a dirty trick? I can't wait to get back at him."

"Come on, Lizzie. You know Sammy probably talked him into it," Maria said. "Sammy's not a bad kid, but you know he loves to play tricks. I don't think he and Charles meant to be mean."

"Still," said Lizzie. She opened the fridge and gazed inside, then pulled out a bottle of ketchup. "I know! When I'm holding Chewy later on, I can pour some of this on my hand and pretend he bit me. It'll look just like blood."

Maria shook her head. "That's not too nice," she said. "I think you should just forgive and

101

forget and move on. Training the puppies and finding them good homes is the most important thing, isn't it?"

"But Mr. Beauregard said it's good to take action when you're mad," Lizzie said, remembering. "That's how our whole idea for the demonstration started." She passed a bone-shaped cookie cutter to Maria, who had just rolled out their first batch of dough.

"Well, maybe when it's a big store you're mad at, or a puppy mill, that's true," said Maria. "But when it's your little brother? Who didn't really do anything *that* terrible?" She raised her eyebrows at Lizzie.

Lizzie knew that Maria always wished she had a brother. As an only child, she saw just the *good* side of having siblings. Sometimes she didn't understand what pests they could be. But Lizzie also knew that Maria was probably right. What good would it do to take revenge on Charles? He obviously felt bad about what he'd done. "You know how Sammy's a bad influence on Charles?" she asked her friend. "Well, I guess you're a *good* influence on me." She put the ketchup bottle back into the fridge.

"Think of it this way," said Maria. "You should be happy, because all those 'mistakes' that Chica had were fake. That means that your Twenty-Minute Plan *works*." She opened the oven and slipped a tray of biscuits in to bake.

Lizzie had to smile. Maria was absolutely right. "Yeah!" She held up a hand for a high five.

Downtown, Charles and Sammy worked hard all day at collecting signatures. They stopped every single person who walked by and told them about puppy mills and why they should be banned and why PetLove shouldn't sell puppies that came from puppy mills. Some people took the time to listen and talk about the problem; some just signed the petition and went on their way; a few people shook their heads and tsk-tsked but didn't seem to want to get involved. Almost everybody petted Chewy and Rufus and Goldie and said what good dogs they were. Charles kept a very, very close eye on Chewy. Fortunately, he did not bite anybody, though he did mouth one lady's hand.

"Sorry," Charles said. "He doesn't mean anything by it."

The lady laughed. "It's fine. I'm used to puppies, even though my dog, Foxie, is all grown up now. I must say, this is one of the cutest puppies I've ever seen. He's tiny, but he has so much personality."

"He's looking for a forever home," Charles said. "He's from a puppy mill near here, but he got rescued. He's really smart and really sweet."

"Ooh." The lady bent over Chewy and cooed to him. "Would you like to come live with me and Foxie? Foxie loves little dogs." She smiled at Charles. "I'll be sure to come to your demonstration tomorrow and bring Foxie. If they get along, this cutie-pie might just have a new home."

Charles grinned at Sammy behind the lady's back.

"Yes!" Sammy crowed when the lady had signed the petition and walked away. "Wait till Lizzie hears. You found Chewy a home. You won the bet!"

But Charles shook his head. "I don't think it's a good idea to tell her until I'm sure." He had seen more than one puppy adoption fall through.

After a few more hours of work, Charles and Sammy had collected almost a hundred signatures. He couldn't wait to show the petition to Lizzie. Would it be enough to make up for the trick he'd played on her?

By the time Charles got home, Lizzie and Maria had baked seven dozen biscuits. "That's enough for eighty-four dogs." Lizzie showed them off to her brother.

"We might need even more than that," said Charles. Proudly, he showed Lizzie the petition.

"Not bad." Lizzie hated to admit it, but Charles had done well. That was a lot of signatures. How could Mr. Sneed ignore that?

Maria shot her a glance. "Why don't you let him collect more signatures at the demonstration?" she whispered.

Lizzie threw up her hands. Wasn't Maria taking this "good influence" thing a little too far? "Okay, okay."

"Yay!" yelled Charles. "I think there will be a ton of people and dogs there. We told everybody about the demonstration, and a lot of them said they'd be there."

"Well, we'll see," said Lizzie. She still wasn't quite ready to forgive Charles for the trick he'd played on her. "I hope they all show up."

CHAPTER NINE

"Yikes! I can't believe they all showed up." Lizzie stared at the crowd gathered in front of PetLove the next morning. Dozens of people and dogs milled around, and more arrived every minute. Lizzie spotted a man peering out the PetLove window. He was wearing a suit jacket over a button-down version of the red PetLove staff T-shirt. "That must be Mr. Sneed!" she said. She smiled at him. He did not smile back.

"We don't have nearly enough signs for everyone to carry," Charles said, beginning to unload a pile of signs from the back of Dad's truck. He and Sammy and Lizzie and Maria had worked together for hours the night before, painting signs with slogans like NO MORE PUPPY

MILLS! and LOVE YOUR PETS? DON'T SHOP AT PETLOVE! Charles had figured that a lot of the people he had talked to the day before would be there. But the crowd this morning was even bigger than he had expected — probably because Mom had mentioned the demonstration in her article, which had come out in that morning's paper.

Charles had not been able to look at the pictures with the article or even read too much of what Mom had written about what she'd seen at the puppy mill. It made him sick to think about all those dogs and puppies locked up in cages. It made him mad, too. And it must have made a lot of other people angry, because here they were, to protest puppy mills. All *kinds* of people, from toddling babies to grandparents with canes. And they'd all brought their dogs. Big dogs, little dogs, fluffy dogs, tough-guy dogs. The people chatted while their dogs sniffed one another. Charles spotted the lady who wanted to adopt Chewy and waved to her. She waved back and pointed to the dog at the end of her leash, a beautiful reddish-gold dog with a fluffy coat. That must be Foxie. The lady smiled at Charles. Yay! Maybe he really would win the bet. As soon as he got the chance, he'd bring Chewy over to meet Foxie.

Ms. Dobbins had arrived early, with Mr. Beauregard. They had brought all the puppy mill puppies from the shelter, piled in Mr. Beauregard's car along with Andrew and Julie. Now Lizzie saw Ms. Dobbins look at the crowd. The shelter director laughed, then turned to give a funny little salute to the man staring out the PetLove window — the same man Lizzie had smiled at earlier. "Too bad for you, Mr. Sneed!" Ms. Dobbins turned back to Charles and Lizzie. "I warned him. I asked him one more time not to sell puppies from the puppy mill. I told him that our Caring Club was planning a demonstration. I don't think he took me very seriously."

Charles and Sammy handed out signs while Mom helped Lizzie and Maria set up the dog-wash station in front of Rispoli's Hardware. Dad and the Bean walked Buddy through the crowd, handing out free homemade dog biscuits. Lizzie and Maria had packaged them in sandwich bags with a recipe card attached. WHY BUY TREATS AT PETLOVE WHEN YOU CAN MAKE THEM YOURSELF? said the heading on the card.

Ms. Dobbins and Mr. Beauregard walked around greeting all the people and their dogs. Charles noticed that Mr. Beauregard had a pat, a kiss, and a few nice words for every dog he met. He paid attention to the dogs while Ms. Dobbins welcomed the owners and thanked them for coming.

"Yow, Chewy!" Charles said. "I mean, yip-yip-yip." He had Chewy in one arm and a load of signs in the other. This was *not* a good time for Chewy to chomp his fingers.

Oops! Sorry! I forgot for a second!

Chewy stopped biting. Instead, he began to struggle in Charles's arms, trying to get down so he could run after the bigger dogs. "Yap-yap-yap!" he barked at the two German shepherds who had arrived with Meg, one of the firefighters who worked with Dad. "Yip-yip-yip!" he howled at Cinnamon and Cocoa, the mixed-breed dogs that the Petersons' author friend Mary Thompson had adopted. "Grr-yip!" Chewy barked at Zeke, a goofy chocolate Lab who belonged to Charles's friend Harry, and Murphy, another chocolate Lab who was a service dog for Harry's friend Dee.

Dee laughed as she rolled her wheelchair along, carrying a sign Charles had given her. "That's one tough little pooch you've got there, Charles."

Chewy even barked at the other puppies from the puppy mill as Andrew and Julie strolled by, carrying signs they'd made themselves. CARING

PAWS: THE BEST PLACE TO FIND A PUPPY TO LOVE! said Andrew's. Julie's read SUPPORT YOUR LOCAL ANIMAL SHELTER. They each struggled to manage three puppies on constantly tangling leashes.

At the dog-wash station, Lizzie and Maria had an assembly-line system going: to the beat of the music that blasted out of speakers they'd set up, Maria wet the dogs down, applied baby shampoo, and lathered them up. Then Lizzie took their leashes and led them through a plastic kiddie pool they'd filled up with water. That was the first rinse. A long blast from the hose finished the job.

People stuffed money into a collection jar Ms. Dobbins had put on the table next to Charles's petition. Most people paid more than two dollars for their dogs to be washed. Lizzie had seen Mr. Beauregard — who didn't even *have* a dog — slip a twenty-dollar bill into the jar. "Check it out," said Lizzie to Maria. "We'll raise a lot of money for the shelter today."

"Caring Club rules!" Maria gave Lizzie a high five, then danced away to hose down the next dog.

"Lizzie!" Mom said. She had come over to bring each of the girls a bottle of juice. "You're a total mess."

Lizzie looked down at herself and laughed. She was covered with suds and soaking wet, not only from the hose but also from all the wet dogs shaking off next to her. Her hair hung down in strings in front of her face, and her sneakers went *squish, squish, squish* with every step she took. She smiled at her mother. "Isn't it great?"

"Well, I'm glad you're enjoying yourself," said Mom. "But I did want you to meet someone very important, and I'm not sure what he'll think of your new look." She waved at a man in a gray suit who walked toward the dog-wash station, inching his way through the long line of dogs. He stopped every few steps to chat with a dog owner or shake a hand. "Over here, Senator!"

Lizzie gasped. Senator Bisbee was here. Perfect. Who cared what she looked like? What mattered was that the senator had come to the demonstration. Now he would see what an important issue this was. He would understand why the state should ban puppy mills forever. She ran to the table to grab the petition and a handful of brochures.

"Senator Bisbee, this is my daughter, Lizzie," Mom said when the senator had picked his way through the mess of dogs and water and suds.

"Well, it's a pleasure to meet you, Lizzie," said the senator.

Lizzie shook his outstretched hand. So *that* was what people meant by a "firm handshake." Ouch!

"So you're the feisty little girl who organized all this?" The senator waved a hand at the crowd.

Little girl? Lizzie bit her lip. "I hardly did anything," she admitted. "It was Mom's article. Plus, my brother Charles told lots of people. He got all these signatures on a petition, too." She handed the petition, which was sort of soggy now, to the senator.

He leafed through the pages, glancing at the names. "Very impressive," he said. Then he caught sight of Chica, who had wriggled her way out of Lizzie's apron pocket and jumped down onto the ground. Chica put both paws up on the senator's leg.

"Chica!" said Mom.

But the senator didn't seem to mind. "My, what a cute puppy. Is it yours, little girl?"

"That's Chica. She came from a puppy mill. She happens to be looking for a forever home."

"Is that so?" The senator squatted down to pet Chica. "Well, aren't you a pretty gal?"

Chica squirmed and wagged and tilted her head in the cutest possible way.

That's right! That's right! You bet I am!

"Aww," said the senator. "I might just have to take you home."

Lizzie and Maria grinned at each other. Yes!

The senator stood up and dusted off the knees of his pants. "Of course, that depends on what my wife says. She'll be here soon."

Lizzie shoved some brochures into his hand. "I'm sure she'll love Chica. And maybe once you adopt her, you'll understand even more why you should support a bill banning puppy mills."

Senator Bisbee chuckled. "You are quite the little spitfire, aren't you?"

Quit calling me little! Lizzie felt like screaming. But for the puppies' sake, she held her tongue. "I just care about animals; that's all." Lizzie swept Chica up and nestled her into her apron pocket.

But the senator had stopped listening. He gazed out over the crowd, waving at one person, winking at another. Lizzie could tell he was getting ready to go shake some more hands. But it didn't matter. She had a feeling he would support their cause. Plus, she had found Chica a terrific forever family. "Can you believe it?" she asked Mom and Maria as Senator Bisbee melted back into the crowd. "He's going to adopt Chica. I won the bet! I *am* the world's best dog trainer." Lizzie held up her fists like a winning athlete.

But Mom shook her head. "I don't know, Lizzie. Sometimes politicians just say the things they think people want to hear."

Lizzie didn't care what Mom thought. She was too happy. She turned up the music and sang along as she danced her way over to the next soapy dog. This was the best demonstration ever.

Charles and Sammy were having a great time, too. They held up their signs and chanted along with a group of marchers who walked around in a big circle right in front of PetLove's entrance.

"No more puppy mills! No more puppy mills!" hollered Charles. Not one customer had gone inside all morning. Mr. Sneed stood by the front window, arms crossed in front of his chest and a big frown on his face. Charles waved and smiled but Mr. Sneed just kept frowning.

A moment later, the well-organized demonstration turned into a total disaster. It all began when Chica started to bark from across the parking lot. Then Chewy joined in.

Where are you? Where are you?

I'm over here! Come find me!

Lots of other dogs began to bark, too. Then Chewy pulled so hard on his leash that it slipped out of Charles's hand. Lizzie must have let go of Chica, too, because two seconds later, Charles saw how two tiny dogs could create big trouble. The Chihuahuas ran through the crowd with leashes dragging. They chased and nipped and barked at every bigger dog they saw — which was just about every dog at the demonstration. The bigger dogs barked back or charged away, dragging their people behind them. Then the Chihuahuas got hold of the hose. They ran with it, spraying the crowd with floods of water.

Charles groaned.

Lizzie and Charles chased after Chica and Chewy, but the little dogs wove and dodged through the crowd. People yelled and screamed as the hose whipped around, soaking everyone and everything. Chewy's ears flapped as he ran, and Chica's eyes were bright with excitement.

What fun! What fun!

Whee!

Lizzie tried to grab Chica, and Charles tried to tackle Chewy.

"Over here!"

"No, this way!"

But no matter how hard they tried, they couldn't capture their wild puppies.

Then Mr. Beauregard stepped out from the middle of the crowd. Calmly, he reached down and scooped up both Chihuahuas. He stuffed Chewy into his right overalls pocket and Chica into his left. "Okay, folks," he boomed in his big foghorn voice. "Let's all just take it easy now. Just a couple of pups having fun, that's all."

CHAPTER TEN

"It's all your fault." Lizzie scowled at Charles as he helped her gather up a bunch of soggy brochures. The demonstration had never quite recovered after everybody had gotten soaked. Most of the people had drifted away, including Maria and Sammy, who had both suddenly remembered things they had to do. Mom was still roaming the parking lot, interviewing the last stragglers for a follow-up story on the demonstration, and Dad had taken the Bean and Buddy back home. Lizzie jabbed a finger at Charles's petition, which drooped halfway off the wet table. Now the heading said *E THE USIGED*. Inky blotches showed where people's signatures had melted away. "You had to go telling everybody about the demonstration," she went on. "If there weren't so many people here, it wouldn't have turned into such a mess."

"If there weren't so many people here, we wouldn't have a hundred ninety-eight signatures on our petition," Charles shot back. "And you wouldn't have raised all that money from the dog wash." He pointed to the jar on the table, which was stuffed with bills. "And did you hear that Ms. Dobbins found homes today for four of the puppy mill puppies?"

Lizzie knew he was right. In a lot of ways, the demonstration had been a success. But she was still mad. "I thought I'd found a home for Chica. Senator Bisbee was all set to take her — until his wife saw what a troublemaker she can be. You should have seen Mrs. Bisbee's face. There's no way they're adopting Chica now." Mrs. Bisbee had been one of the first people to disappear when the demonstration had gotten out of control.

"Well," said Charles, "I didn't tell you before, but I thought I had found a home for Chewy, too." He told Lizzie about the lady who owned Foxie. He hadn't even had the chance to talk to her before things got crazy. But he'd seen her and Foxie scrambling to avoid the wildly spraying hose. "She didn't even bother to come over and say anything. And I bet she won't call, either. She grabbed Foxie and left before I could stop her."

Lizzie plopped down on a chair, her arms folded tightly across her chest. "What a disaster," she said. "That's the last demonstration *I* ever plan."

Chica scampered up onto Lizzie's lap and licked her chin.

Cheer up, cheer up! Soon it'll be dinnertime!

Lizzie gave Chica a scratch between the ears. "I know. Who wants to go live with that silly old senator, anyway? But we do have to find you a home."

"Silly old senator? Are you referring to me?" Lizzie looked up to see Senator Bisbee standing there, with Mom beside him.

Lizzie coughed. She felt her face grow warm and knew she was blushing. But the senator just smiled. "I came back to give you some *good* news," he said. His chest puffed out and he looked into the distance as if he were making a speech to thousands of people, even though his only audience was Mom, Lizzie, and Charles. "I want you to know that I intend to do everything I can to ban these puppy mill operations in this state. I saw today that a lot of people care, really care, about this issue. They signed the petition; they turned up to let their voices be heard. I want them to know that I hear them loud and clear. That's what I do. I listen to the people. Then I try to change things."

Then he relaxed and smiled down at Lizzie and Charles. "I was going to wait to say so until my next official press conference, but your mother here convinced me to tell you right away."

Mom, who stood just behind the senator, gave Lizzie and Charles a big smile and a thumbs-up.

"Wow!" Lizzie turned to Charles, then back to Senator Bisbee. "That's great news."

Charles just beamed.

Then the senator had to ruin it all. He nodded wisely. "It just shows what one determined little girl and boy can do."

Ugh. "Little" again. But Lizzie didn't even care. She felt terrific.

"Senator, I have one more question for you." Mom flipped open her reporter's notebook. "Can you give me a timetable —"

They strolled away to finish their interview.

Lizzie and Charles smacked a big high five. "Yes!" they yelled.

A few minutes later, as Lizzie was wiping down a PetLove window that had gotten sprayed, she heard someone come up behind her.

When she turned around, she saw Mr. Sneed standing there. Was he going to yell at her? He held up his hands and smiled a thin smile. "I surrender," he said. "You folks win. I haven't had a customer all day. I guess people really do care about this issue. I'll talk to that Ms. Dobbins woman first thing tomorrow, and arrange to take her shelter animals instead of those puppies from the puppy mill. Happy?"

Lizzie and Charles were speechless. They stared openmouthed as Mr. Sneed turned on his heel and walked off. Then Lizzie managed to find her voice. "Thank you!" she called. "If you want to let everybody know, you can tell that reporter over there. She'll put it in tomorrow's paper!"

"Well, well, well." Mr. Beauregard strolled over a few moments later to talk to Charles and Lizzie. "From what I've seen, I can guess that you two might be feeling pretty good right now." He gestured to Mr. Sneed and the senator, who both stood talking to Mom by the shopping cart–return area.

So, Charles thought, *he's been watching.* Funny — Charles had been watching Mr. Beauregard, too. He had obviously had a great time at the demonstration. Why? Because he loved dogs. Charles could tell. He had pointed it out to Lizzie, too. Mr. Beauregard had visited with all the dogs at the demonstration, stopping to pet them and talk to them and scratch their heads. Sometimes he even squatted right down to give a dog a big hug or a kiss and whisper into its ear.

Mr. Beauregard had stayed around until the very last dog had left — except for Chewy and Chica, of course. Now he pulled out his checkbook. "Have you counted how much you earned, soaping up all those mutts?" he asked. "I intend to write a check that matches the amount. That way, we'll double the donation to Caring Paws."

"Really?" Charles stared at him. What was it like to be so rich that you could just *do* that? He tilted his head. "So, do you have a private plane and everything?" he asked.

"*Charles*," said Lizzie in a "don't be so nosy" voice. She pulled her chair up to the table and dumped all the money out of the jar so she could count it.

But Mr. Beauregard was nodding. "I sure do," he said. "I have to, in order to see after all my businesses. They're based all over the world."

"So," Charles said casually, "if you had, say, two teeny, tiny dogs that you wanted to take with you, it would be no problem. Not like it would be on a regular plane."

"Ha! I guess you're right about that. I can pretty much do whatever I want. I own the plane, after all." Mr. Beauregard shoved back his red baseball cap and laughed.

Charles didn't have to say anything to Lizzie or even give her a look. She knew just what he was up to. She stopped counting money and joined right in. "Chewy and Chica are so smart," she told Mr. Beauregard. "We've taught them a lot, but they've learned from each other, too. Like, Chewy taught Chica about a good place to pee out in our yard, and Chica is always teaching Chewy that it hurts if he bites. They're both good dogs, but together, they're *great*."

"Plus, they really like you," Charles said. "They calmed down so fast when you put them in your pockets. Chewy likes some people, and Chica likes others, but there're only a very few people that they both love."

Mr. Beauregard laughed again. "Well, my dear old mother always did used to say that I had a way with dogs."

"That first day we met you, when you bought all the puppies from that truck," Charles said, "you said you wished you could keep them all. How about just keeping two? *These* two?" He reached down to pick up Chewy.

Lizzie picked up Chica. "What do you think?"

Charles and Lizzie held out the puppies. Chewy's tiny foot pawed the air, and Chica let out a "yip-yip-yip."

Take us! Take us!

Please! I love it in your pocket!

Mr. Beauregard let out a huge booming laugh. "Oh, why not?" he said. "They're no bigger than a couple of fleas. I can fit 'em in my briefcase, if I have to." He reached out his long, skinny hands, and gently, he took the puppies. Cradling one in each hand, he beamed down at them. "My new best pals," he said. "Everybody needs a friend when they're out on the road."

Mom came over when she heard everybody laughing. Lizzie and Charles told her what had happened. "Wow, great news," she said. "You two really get the job done when you're not busy squabbling, don't you?" She gave them a meaningful look, and they knew exactly what she was thinking. The bet had made them so competitive that they had forgotten to work together. "It's been a pretty good day all around," Mom went on. "And now I get to tell your dad to start cleaning out that junk drawer."

"Yay, Mom!" Lizzie and Charles cheered. Neither of them really cared that their own bet had ended in a tie and they would still be doing their same old chores. The main thing was that Chewy and Chica had found a fantastic forever home.

On the way home, Mom told Lizzie and Charles that now that Mr. Beauregard had adopted Chewy and Chica, there was still time to go up to AdventureLand for a day or two. "Maria and Sammy can come along, too," she said. "You both worked so hard with those dogs, and you deserve a treat."

In the backseat of the van, Charles looked at Lizzie. She looked back at him. "I don't know," Charles said. "I kind of miss Buddy. I feel like I hardly got to play with him all week."

"Same here," said Lizzie. "Plus, I know Ms. Dobbins could still use some extra help over at the shelter. How about if we just stick around home and" — she winked at Charles — "figure out what's next for the Caring Club?"

"Sounds good. No more demonstrations for a while, though, okay?" Mom smiled into the rear-view mirror.

"Fine with me," said Charles. "I bet we can come up with some other great idea."

"I bet you're right," said Lizzie. They grinned at each other and shook on it.

Puppy Tips

What can *you* do to help animals? Maybe you can start your own Caring Club, like Lizzie did. But there are lots of other ways, too. Is your birthday coming up? Some kids ask their friends to donate to the local animal shelter instead of giving presents. If you are old enough, you might be able to volunteer at a shelter. You can help spread the word about animals in trouble by writing letters to the editor of your local newspaper. And of course you can take good care of your own pets. That means making sure that they are clean and healthy, that they have plenty of food and water and a safe, warm place to live, and that they get the training and exercise they need. And don't forget: more than anything, dogs need love. Hug your dog!

Dear Reader,

Like Lizzie, I have always been a "big-dog person." Big dogs are so huggable, and you can take them along on a swim or a run. My favorite breed is black Lab. But as I was writing this book, I learned that Chihuahuas can make terrific pets. They are smart, loyal, easy to take along anywhere you go, and of course very, very cute. I fell in love with Chewy and Chica. I hope you will, too!

Danielle, the woman who designed my website, adopted a Chihuahua. named Luna. Luna's first owner was a friend who became allergic to dogs. Danielle sends her friend pictures of Luna every day.

Yours from the Puppy Place,
Ellen Miles

P.S. If you think Chewy and Chica make a good pair, check out Maggie and Max!

Today was Picture Day at Bowser's Backyard, Aunt Amanda's doggy day care center — and Lizzie was there to help. Katana, a professional photographer, had come to take pictures of all of Aunt Amanda's regular customers — at least, the ones whose owners were interested in paying for a professional portrait of their pet. Which was just about everyone.

Aunt Amanda got the dogs to sit. Katana adjusted her lights, focused her camera, and gave Lizzie the signal. Lizzie squeezed the squeaky toy.

Some dogs stayed put and posed for the camera.

Some dogs — namely, Pugsley — got up and zoomed around the room, dodging everyone who tried to catch them and nearly knocking over Katana's fancy lights.

And a few dogs lay down and went to sleep while Katana was focusing her camera.

Lizzie barely stopped laughing all afternoon. "This is so much fun!" she told Katana. "If you ever need an assistant on your jobs, let me know!"

Finally, Aunt Amanda brought in the very last dog. "This is Baxter," she said, as she led an energetic brown puppy into the room. "After we take his picture, we'll try for a group shot. That should be interesting!"

Lizzie did not recognize Baxter. He was a beautiful puppy, with soft chestnut curls, a white chest, floppy ears, and a sweet, friendly face all covered in curly fur. He bounded happily over to greet Lizzie, pulling Aunt Amanda along behind him. "Hello there, Baxter!" Lizzie squatted down to rub his floppy ears and kiss his sweet black nose. His fur was silky-soft and he smelled delicious. "What breed are you, cutie?" Lizzie pictured the "Dog Breeds of the World" poster she had hanging in her room. Which dog looked most like Baxter?

Aunt Amanda started to say something, but Lizzie stopped her. "Wait," she said, holding up her hand. "Don't tell me! I bet I can guess. Is he a Portuguese water dog?" Lizzie asked.

Aunt Amanda burst out laughing. "Amazing! You have really studied up on your dog breeds. You're never wrong!" She bent down to pet Baxter. "Yes, Baxter here is a Portie, or a PWD, as some people call them."

ABOUT THE AUTHOR

Ellen Miles likes to write about the different personalities of dogs. She is the author of more than 30 books, including the Puppy Place and Taylor-Made Tales series as well as *The Pied Piper* and other Scholastic Classics. Ellen loves to be outdoors every day, walking, biking, skiing, or swimming, depending on the season. She also loves to read, cook, explore her beautiful state, and hang out with friends and family. She lives in Vermont.

If you love animals, be sure to read all the adorable stories in the Puppy Place series!